Old and New Church Music

By

E. T. A. Hoffmann

British Library Cataloguing-in-Publication Data
A catalogue record for this book is available from the
British Library

E. T. A. Hoffman

Ernst Theodor Wilhelm Hoffmann was born in Königsberg, East Prussia in 1776. His family were all jurists, and during his youth he was initially encouraged to pursue a career in law. However, in his late teens Hoffman became increasingly interested in literature and philosophy, and spent much of his time reading German classicists and attending lectures by, amongst others, Immanuel Kant.

In was in his twenties, upon moving with his uncle to Berlin, that Hoffman first began to promote himself as a composer, writing an operetta called Die Maske and entering a number of playwriting competitions. Hoffman struggled to establish himself anywhere for a while, flitting between a number of cities and dodging the attentions of Napoleon's occupying troops. In 1808, while living in Bamberg, he began his job as a theatre manager and a music critic, and Hoffman's break came a year later, with the publication of Ritter Gluck. The story centred on a man who meets, or thinks he has met, a long-dead composer, and played into the 'doppelgänger' theme – at that time very popular in literature. It was shortly after this that Hoffman began to use the pseudonym E. T. A. Hoffmann, declaring the 'A' to stand for 'Amadeus', as a tribute to the great composer, Mozart.

Over the next decade, while moving between Dresden, Leipzig and Berlin, Hoffman produced a great range of both literary and musical works. Probably Hoffman's most well-known story, produced in 1816, is 'The Nutcracker and the Mouse King', due to the fact that – some seventy-six years later - it inspired Tchaikovsky's ballet The Nutcracker.

In the same vein, his story 'The Sandman' provided both the inspiration for Léo Delibes's ballet Coppélia, and the basis for a highly influential essay by Sigmund Freud, called 'The Uncanny'. (Indeed, Freud referred to Hoffman as the "unrivalled master of the uncanny in literature.")

Alcohol abuse and syphilis eventually took a great toll on Hoffman though, and – having spent the last year of his life paralysed – he died in Berlin in 1822, aged just 46. His legacy is a powerful one, however: He is seen as a pioneer of both Romanticism and fantasy literature, and his novella, Mademoiselle de Scudéri: A Tale from the Times of Louis XIV is often cited as the first ever detective story.

Old and New Church Music

Vincent and Sylvester having joined the Brotherhood, Lothair delivered a long harangue to them, in which he set forth, in most entertaining fashion, at great length, and with much minuteness, the duties incumbent upon a true Serapion Brother. "And now," he concluded, "give me your solemn word, dear and worthy novices of our Order, confirming the same by solemn handgrip, that you will faithfully observe and follow the rule of Saint Serapion; that is to say, that you will, at all times, and in all circumstances, devote your every endeavour to be--at the meetings of the Brotherhood--as genial, witty, kindly, and sympathetic as may be in your power."

"I, for my part," said Vincent, "enter into this undertaking with all my heart. I mean to pay over my entire stock of brains and imagination into the coffers of the Brotherhood; expecting to be therefrom, at all times, and on all occasions, not only fed and supported, but actually crammed. On every occasion when I purpose to come among you I shall--according to the proverb--give my ape a full allowance of sugar, that he may be sufficiently primed for the execution of the merriest capers. And, inasmuch as our patron saint has acquired his fame and glory from a decided quantum of insanity, I shall copy him, in this respect, to the utmost of my power, so that the Brotherhood may never have to complain of an absence of this important element of their being. I am prepared, if that should be your desire, to dish you up a most varied and extensive assortment of the most interesting 'fixed ideas.' I can imagine myself to be a Roman emperor, like Professor Titel; or a cardinal, like Father Scambati. I can believe, like the woman mentioned by Trallianus, that the universe is upheld upon my left thumb; or that my nose is made of glass, and irradiates the walls and the ceiling with beautiful prismatic colours. Also, I can think I am a looking-glass, like the little Scotchman, Donald Munro, and reflect, and copy all the glances, grimaces, and postures of those who look into my face. More than this, I feel capable of convincing myself, as the Chevalier D'Epernay did, that my anima sensitiva has shorn my head bare, so that I shall merely have to rely upon the hair or two left on my lips to inspire you with a certain amount of respect. As true Serapion brethren, you will know how to indulge, and give due honour to all these little delusions. And pray don't think of curing me, by applying the remedies recommended by Boerhaave, Mercurialis, Antius of Amyda, Friedrich Kraft, and Herr Richter; inasmuch as they all prescribe a considerable amount of castration, or, at all events, gentle slapping of the face, and boxing of the ears. And the fact is, without doubt, that a certain amount of threshing has a beneficial effect on both heart and mind, and awakens the activity of some of the most important functions of the body. I just ask you, what would have become of us--should we ever have learnt a single one of our lessons, in the fifth form, but for a due amount of threshing? I recollect quite well that when, at

8

the age of twelve, I read the 'Sorrows of Werther,' I went off and immediately fell in love with a young lady of thirteen, and wanted to shoot myself. Luckily my father cured me of this super-excitation of my heart on the system of treatment recommended by Rhases and Valuscus de Taranta, who prescribed castigation as a sovereign remedy for love. At the same time the old gentleman shed warm, paternal tears of joy on discovering that I was not an ass: for experience proves that love, in said animal, increases in proportion as he is beaten."

"Oh, most delightful of all fabulists!" cried Theodore. "How you are caprioling and curvetting! Please to go on doing so always! Flash your lightnings in amongst us whenever the atmosphere is growing sultry, in all the quaintest of your phrases. And, above all, freshen our Sylvester up a little; for, after his usual wont, he has not uttered a single word as yet."

"The fact is," said Ottmar, "that I can scarcely convince myself that it really is Sylvester who is sitting in that chair, smiling at us so benignantly. It seems to me almost incredible that he can have come away, so soon from his country dwelling, which he so much preferred to our city life; and I keep believing that he is merely some pleasing apparition, presently to vanish from our sight amongst those clouds which he is blowing from his cigar."

"Heaven forefend!" cried Sylvester, laughing. "Do you suppose that a quiet, happy personage, such as I am, has assumed the form of an enchanter, and is deluding honest folks with his mere simulacrum? Do you think I have anything of the Philadelphia, or the Swedenborg about me? If you blame me for my silence, Theodore, let me say that I am sparing my breath because I want to read you a story, suggested to me by one of Kolbe's pictures, which I wrote during my long stay in the country. If it surprises you, Ottmar, that I have come back here, although I am so fond of the quiet and the leisure of the country, remember that, though the constant turmoil, and the endless, empty business of this great town are uncongenial to my whole nature, still, if I am to turn my being a poet and a writer to any account, I stand in need of many incitements which I can meet with here only. The tale which I wish to read to you--and which I believe to possess a certain amount of merit--would never have been written if I had not seen Kolbe's picture at the Exhibition, and then worked the affair out in the quiet of the country."

"Sylvester is right," said Lothair, "in seeking--as a writer of plays and tales--suggestions and incitements in the whirl of city life, and then in giving quiet leisure to his mind, in which to work those suggestions out. Of course he might have seen the picture in the country; but he would not have seen, there, the living characters whom it inspired with life and movement, and into whom the people portrayed in the picture passed and entered. A poet such as he is ought not to retire into solitude. He ought to live in the most stirring and varied society, so as to see, and grasp, its endlessly manifold aspects."

"Ha!" cried Vincent, "as Jaques, in 'As You Like It,' calls out when he sees Touchstone,

10

'A fool, a fool! I met a fool i' the forest,

A motley fool; oh, lamentable world!'

So I cry 'a poet! a poet! I met a poet! He came stumbling out of the third wineshop at high noon, looked up with his moist, drunken eyes at the sun, and cried, in his inspiration "Oh, sweet, gentle moon, how fall thy rays upon my heart, illumining, in marvellous sort, that universe which lives and moves within this soul of mine. Lead on before me, thou brave luminary, that I may steer my course to where experience of life and knowledge of mankind stream towards my ken, in rich abundance, for advantageous employment! Character-studies, lifelike drawing--not possible without living models! Glorious drink! Noble, splendid ardour, opening the heart and kindling the fancy! Yes, that man eating sausages in there lives within my soul! He is tall and lean, has on a blue frock coat with gilt buttons, English boots, takes snuff out of a black lacquered snuff-box, speaks German fluently, and is consequently a German, in spite of his boots and the Italian sausages; a glorious, lifeful German character for my next novel! But, more knowledge of mankind! More character!"' And with that my poet sailed, with a fair wind, into the harbour of the fourth wineshop."

"Stop! you Oliver Martext," cried Lothair. "I call you so, because you have completely marred my text. I know well enough what you are driving at with your poet who collects experience of life in wineshops, and by his man in the blue frock coat; and I don't care to expatiate further on the Thema. But there are other, very different, people too, who think that,

11

when they have accurately described the personality of this or that unimportant 'subject' they have drawn a strikingly life-like character. The peculiar pigtail which this or that old man wears--the colours in which this or that girl dresses--are not enough. It requires a certain special faculty, and a penetrating eye, to see the forms of life in their deeper individuality. And even this seeing is not enough. It is the poet's spirit--that spirit which dwells within every true poet--which brings the pictures which he has seen, in their endlessly, infinitely, varied changefulness, as they have shown themselves to him--on to the stage. And then, by a process like chemical precipitation, those forms appear as substrata belonging to life and the world in their complete extension. Such are those wonderful characters--wholly unconnected with place and time--whom every one knows, and looks upon as friends, who move on amongst us for ever, in perfect fulness of life. Need I instance Sancho Panza and Falstaff? And as you, Vincent, spoke of a blue frock coat, it is rather curious that forms, which a true poet has drawn in the way I have just instanced, appear to costume themselves of their own accord, just in the way most appropriate to their characters."

"Yes," said Ottmar, "and that is the case in actual life as well. Doubtless we have all felt most distinctly, with respect to characters we have met, that those people could not have been dressed differently, to be in keeping with their inner being; that such and such a man could not have had on another sort of hat or coat than he actually had. That this is the case is not so wonderful, as that we should see that it is so."

"But don't you think it is only because we notice it, that it happens?" interrupted Cyprian.

"Oh! unapproachable subtlety!" cried Vincent.

"I cordially agree with all that Lothair has maintained on this subject," cried Sylvester. "Don't forget, however, that--besides our meetings and conversations--there is another source of enjoyment which I miss in the country--one which greatly penetrates and elevates me. I mean the musical performances, the renderings of the glorious works of musicians. This very day I heard Beethoven's Mass in C in the Catholic Church. It made a deep impression on me."

"And that," said Cyprian, moodily, "does not surprise me, just because to have to do without things of the kind makes one enjoy them the more. Hunger is the best sauce. To speak candidly, Beethoven--in his Mass in C--has given us a very charming, I may, perhaps, say a genial, work; but it is not a Mass. Where is the strict ecclesiastical style?"

"I know, Cyprian," said Theodore, "you only care for the old composers, and are horrified at the sight of a black note in a church-score; and that you are unjustly strict and severe in your opinions about the more modern church music."

"At the same time," said Lothair, "I think there is too much of the jubilant--of earthly rejoicing--in Beethoven's Mass. I should very much like to know wherein the utter diverseness of the spirit in which the masters have composed the different portion of the Mass lies; they contrast with each other in their treatment of it so completely!"

"Exactly," said Sylvester, "that is what has so often struck me, too, as inexplicable. One would suppose, for example, that the words, 'Benedictus qui venit in nomine domini' could only be set in the same sort of pious, tranquil style. Yet, I not only know that they have been set in the most diverse manners by the greatest masters, but also that--penetrated by the most diverse feelings--I can never think the setting of them, by this or by the other great writer, to be in any way a mistake. Theodore might, perhaps, enlighten us to this."

"I should be glad to do so as far as I can," said Theodore, "but I should have to deliver a little lecture on the subject, and I fear it would be too serious to fit well in with the facetious tone in which our conversation began."

"It is true Serapionism that jest and earnest should alternate," said Ottmar; "so please to deliver yourself confidently, Theodore, on a subject in which we are all so deeply interested; except, perhaps, Vincent, who knows nothing about music."

Theodore accordingly went on, as follows:

"Prayer and worship doubtless affect the mind according to its predominant, or even momentary, mood, or tuning-- as this results from physical or mental well-being, comfort, happiness, or suffering. So that, at one time, prayer or worship is inward contrition--even to self-despite and shame, grovelling in the dust before the lightnings of the Lord of the worlds, angry with the sinner; and, at another time, vigorous elevation towards the infinite; child-like trust in the mercy of the Omnipotent, anticipation of the

14

promised bliss. The words of the Mass present--in their cycle--merely the occasion--the opportunity--or, at highest, the clue, for devotion, and will awaken the due concord in the soul, according to its frame of thought at the time. In the Kyrie, God's mercy is implored; the Gloria celebrates His omnipotence and majesty; the Credo gives expression to the faith on which the pious soul firmly builds; and after--in the Sanctus and the Benedictus--the holiness of God has been exalted, and blessings promised to those who approach Him in confident faith; prayer is offered, in the Agnus and the Dona, to the Mediator, that He may send down His peace and gladness to the believing soul. Now even (to begin with), on account of this very universality (which in no way encroaches upon the inner significance, and the deeper application which each one lays into it, according to his own peculiar condition of mind and conscience), the text lends and adapts itself to the most infinite variety of musical treatment; and this is the reason why there are Kyries, Glorias, &c., so widely dissimilar in character, tone, and the rest. For instance, one has but to compare the Kyries in Haydn's Masses in C major and D minor; also his Benedictuses. From this it follows that the composer who (as ought always to be the case) sets to work, inspired with true devoutness, to write a Mass, will let the individual religious attunement of his own mind predominate (all the words being ready to adapt themselves to that); not suffering himself to be led away in the Miserere, the Gloria, Qui Tollis, and so forth, into a many-tinted medley of the most heart-rending sorrow of the contrite heart, with jubilant clangour and jingle. All works of the latter sort, which, in recent times, there have been numbers of, carpentered together in the most frivolous fashion, are abortions, engendered by impure minds; and I reject them just as unhesitatingly as Cyprian does. But I render deep admiration to the glorious church compositions of Michael and Joseph Haydn, Hasse, Neumann, and others, not forgetting the old works of the pious Italian masters, Leo, Durante, Benevoli, Perli, and others, whose lofty, beautiful, noble simplicity, whose wonderful power of impressing the very depths of the soul by their simple modulations, wholly devoid of strikingness of display, seem to constitute an art which is altogether lost in recent (and most recent,) times. Without desiring to adhere to the early, primitive, pure church style, merely because what is holy disdains the varied dress of mundane niceties of subtlety, one cannot--to begin with--doubt that simple music has a better effect, musically speaking, in churches, than that which is elaborate; for the more rapidly notes succeed one another the more they are lost in the lofty spaces of buildings, so that the whole effect becomes confused and unintelligible. Hence, in a measure, the grand effect of Chorales in church. I unconditionally agree with you, Cyprian, as to the superiority of the noble church music of ancient times over that of recent date, just on account of its constantly maintaining its truly holy style. At the same time, I think that the richness and fulness which music has gained in more recent times--chiefly by the introduction of instruments--should be made use of in

16

churches, not to produce mere idle display, but in a noble and worthy manner. Perhaps the bold simile--that the old church music of the Italians holds somewhat the same relation to that of the more modern Germans as Saint Peter's at Rome holds to Strasburg Cathedral--may not be inapt. The grandiose proportions of Saint Peter's elevate the mind, because it finds them commensurable; but the beholder gazes with a strange inward disquiet upon the Strasburg Minster, as it soars aloft in the most daring curves, and the most wondrous interfacings of varied, fantastic forms and ornamentation. And this very unrest awakens a sense of the Unknown, the Marvellous; and the spirit readily yields itself to this dream, in which it seems to recognise the Super-earthly, the Unending. Now this is exactly the effect of that purely romantic element which pervades Mozart and Haydn's compositions. It is easy to see that it would not, now, be a very simple matter for a composer to write a church composition in the lofty, simple style of the old Italians. Without saying that the real, pious faith which gave to those masters the power to proclaim the holiest of the holy in those earnest, noble strains may probably seldom dwell in the hearts of artists in more modern times, it is enough to refer to that incapacity which results from the lack of true genius, and, similarly, from the absence of self-renunciation. Is it not in the most absolute simplicity that real genius plies its pinions the most wonderfully? But who does not take delight in letting the treasure which he possesses glitter before the eyes of all? Who is content with the approval of the rare

17

knowers--the few in whose eyes that which is truly good and successful work is the more precious--or rather, the only precious, work? The reason why there is scarcely what can be termed 'a style' remaining, is that people have everywhere taken to employing the same means of expression. We often hear solemn Themas stalking majestically along in comic operas, playful little ditties in opera seria, and masses and oratorios of operatic cut in the churches. Now the proper application--ecclesiastically--of musical figuration, and all the resources of instrumentation, demands a rare degree of genius, and an exceptional profundity of intellect. Mozart--gallant and courtier-like as he is in his two well-known Masses in C major--has, nevertheless, solved this problem magnificently in his Requiem. For that is romantic sacred music, proceeding from the depths of the master's heart and soul; and I have no need to say how finely Haydn, too, speaks in his Masses of the highest and holiest things; although he cannot be acquitted of a good deal of trifling--writing for writing's sake--here and there. As soon as I knew that Beethoven had written a Mass, and before I had heard or read a note of it, I felt certain that, as regards the style and general moulding, the master had taken old Joseph Haydn as his model. Yet I found I was wrong, as regards the manner in which he had apprehended the text of the Mass. His genius generally prefers to employ the levers of awe and terror; so, thought I, the vision of the super-earthly will have filled his soul with awe, and this is what he will speak out in his music. On the contrary, the whole work expresses a mind filled with childlike clearness and happiness, which, building on its purity, confides in faith on the grace of God, and prays to Him as to a father who wills the best for his children, and hears their petitions. From this point of view, the general character of the composition, its inner structure, and intelligent instrumentation, are quite worthy of the master's genius, when considered as a composition meant to be employed in the service of the Church."

"Still," urged Cyprian, "that point of view is, in my opinion, a wrong one altogether, capable of leading to desecration of the highest things. Let me explain my views about church music, and you will see that I am, at all events, clear on the subject in my own mind. What I think is, that no art proceeds so thoroughly out of the spiritualization of mankind, and demands such pure and spiritual modes and means of expression, as music. The sense of the existence of what is highest and holiest, of that spiritual power which kindles the life of all nature, utters itself audibly in music, which--(at all events vocal music)--is the expression of the highest fulness of existence, i.e., the praise of the Creator. Wherefore, as regards its special inner life, music is an act of religious service, and its fountain-head is to be sought, and to be found, only in religion in the Church. Passing thence onwards into life, ever richer and mightier, music poured forth its inexhaustible treasures over mankind, so that even the secular (or, as it is sometimes styled, the 'profane') might, in childlike delight, adorn itself in that splendour wherewith music illuminated life, through and through, even in all its little, petty, mundane relations. But, when thus adorned, even the secular appeared to be longing for the heavenly, higher realm, and striving to enter in amidst its phenomena. Just by reason of this, its special peculiarity of nature, music could not be the property of the antique world, where everything proceeded from corporalization manifest to the senses; it had to be reserved for more modern times. The two opposite artistic poles of Heathenism and Christianity are Sculpture and Music. Christianity destroyed the former and created the latter (along with painting, which is nearest akin to it). In painting, the ancients knew neither perspective nor colouring; in music, neither melody nor harmony (I use the word 'melody' here in its highest sense, to express an uttering of inward feeling, without reference to words and their rhythmic relationships). But beyond this particular imperfection, which may perhaps indicate only the narrower footing upon which music and painting at that time stood, the germs of those arts could not develop themselves in that unfruitful soil; not until the advent of Christianity could they grow gloriously, and bring forth flowers and fruit in luxurious profusion. Both music and painting maintained their place only in appearance in the antique world; they were kept down by the power of sculpture, or rather they could take no adequate form amid the mighty masses of sculpture. Both those arts were not in the least what we now call 'music' and 'painting.' Just so sculpture disappeared from bodily life by means of the Christian tendency which strives against all corporeal embodiment to the senses, volatilising this into what is spiritual. But the very earliest germ of the music of the present day (in which was enclosed a holy mystery, solveable only by the Christian world), could serve the ancients only according to its essential characteristic specialty, namely, as religious cult. For nothing else were, in those earliest times, their dramas, which were festal representations of the joys and sorrows of a god. The declamation of those dramas was supported by instrumental accompaniments, and even this fact proves that the music of the ancients was purely rhythmic, were it not otherwise demonstrable that (as I have said already) melody and harmony, the two pivots on which our modern music moves, were quite unknown to them. Therefore, though Ambrosius, and afterwards Gregory, based Christian hymns, about the year 1591, on ancient hymns, and that we come upon the traces of that purely rhythmic music in what are called the 'Canto Fermo' and the 'Antiphones,' this is nothing but that they made use of germs which had been handed down to them. And it is certain that a deeper study of that ancient music can interest only the curious antiquary. Whereas, for the practical musician, the most sacred depths of his glorious, truly Christian art were laid open only when Christianity was shining in its brightest splendour in Italy, and the mighty masters, in the consecration of the highest inspiration, proclaimed the holiest mysteries of religion, in tones before unheard. It is noticeable that, not long afterwards, when Guido D'Arezzo had penetrated deeper into the mysteries of the musical art, that art was misunderstood by the uncomprehending, and thought to be a subject for mathematical speculation, so that its true essence was utterly misapprehended, just as it was barely commencing to unfold itself. The marvellous tones of this spiritual language were awakened, and went sounding forth over the world. The means of seizing them and holding them fast were discovered. The 'hieroglyphics' of music (consisting as it does of an intertwining of melody and harmony) were invented; I mean, the mode of writing down music in notes. But soon this mode of indication passed cm rent for the tiling indicated; the masters sunk themselves in harmonic subtleties, and in this manner music, distorted into a speculative science, would have ceased to be music when those subtleties should have attained their highest development. Worship was desecrated by that which was upon it under the name if music, although, to the heart penetrated by that holy art, music itself was alone the true 'worship.' So that there could be but a brief contest, which ended by the glorious victory of an eternal verity over the untrue. Just when Pope Marcellus the Second was on the point of expelling all music from the Church, and so depriving divine worship of its most glorious adornment, the great Master Palestrina revealed to him the sacred mystery and wonder of the tone-art in its most individual and specially characteristic qualities. And from that time music became the most specific feature of the 'Cultus' of the Catholic Church. Thus it was that at that time the most profound comprehension of the true inward life of music dawned and brightened in the masters' pious hearts, and their inimitable, immortal compositions streamed from their souls in holy inspiration. You, Theodore, well know that the Mass for six voices, which Palestrina at that time--I think it was in 1555--composed, in order that the angry Pontiff might hear real music, became widely known by the title of 'Missa Papae Marcelli.' With Palestrina commenced, indisputably, the most glorious era of ancient ecclesiastical music, and, consequently, of all music. This lasted for nearly two hundred years, maintaining its pristine pious dignity and forcibility, although it cannot be denied that, even in the first century after Palestrina, that lofty, inimitable simplicity and dignity lost itself to some extent in a certain 'elegance' which the composers began to aim at. What a master is Palestrina! Without the smallest ornament, without anything approaching melodic sweep, his works consist mainly of chords of the simplest kind, succeeding each other in perfect concords of chords of the triad, by the forcibility and the boldness of which consonances the mind is grasped with indescribable might, and lifted up to the very highest love: i.e., the attunement and consonance of the spiritual with nature (as promised to the Christian), speaks itself out in the chord, which, consequently, came first into existence under the Christian 'dispensation.' So that the chord, and harmony (in contradistinction to mere melody), are the images and expressions of spiritual union, and communion of union, and incorporation with the eternal, the ideal, which thrones above us, and yet encompasses and surrounds us. Therefore the holiest, purest, most ecclesiastical music must be that which flows from the soul as the uncontaminated expression of the love in question, disregarding, nay despising, all that is mundane. And such are Palestrina's simple, majestic compositions, which, conceived in the highest fervour of piety and love, proclaim the godlike with might and glory. To his music truly applies what the Italians apply to the writings of many composers who are shallow and miserable compared to him; it is, of a truth, 'music of another world'--musica dell' altro mondo. Successions of consonant perfect chords of the triad have nowadays become so strange and unfamiliar to us, in our effeminacy, that many an one whose soul is wholly closed to the holy sees nothing in them but helpless unskilfulness of technical construction. But, looking away from those higher considerations, and adverting merely to what we are used to call 'effect,' it is clear as day (as you said already, Theodore), that, in a church, in a great resonant building, everything in the nature of the blending of chord with chord by means of 'transition notes,' weakens the power of the music. In Palestrina's music each chord strikes upon the listener with all its force; the most elaborate modulations could never affect the mind as do those bold, weighty chords, which burst upon us like dazzling beams of light. Palestrina is simple, true, childlike in piety; as strong and mighty, as genuinely Christian in his works as are, in painting, Pietro of Cortona and Albrecht Duerer. For him composition was an act of religion. But I do not forget the great masters Caldara, Barnabei, Scarlatti, Marcello, Lotti, Porpora, Bernardo, Leo, Valotti, and others, who all kept themselves simple, dignified, and forcible. Vividly, at this moment, awakes in me the remembrance of that Mass of Alessandro Scarlatti's for seven voices, 'Alla Capella,' which you, Theodore, once had sung by your own good pupils under your own conductorship. It is a model specimen of the true, grand, and powerful ecclesiastical style, although it has a commencement of the melodic 'swing' which music had acquired by the time it was written, 1705."

"And the mighty Haendel," said Theodore, "the inimitable Hasse, the profound and thoughtful Sebastian Bach; have you not a thought for them?"

"Certainly," answered Cyprian; "I reckon them among the sacred bands whose hearts were strengthened by the power of faith and love. It was this power which brought to them that inspiration by virtue of which they entered into communion with the Highest, and were fired to those works which serve not worldly aims, but are, of necessity, nothing but praise of, and honour to, the loftiest things. This is why those works of theirs bear the impress of veracious truth, and why no anxious striving after 'effect,' no laboured apings of other things, defile and desecrate that of the Heavenly which has revealed itself to them, pure, and clear, and undefiled. This is why there is, in their writings, none of those so-called 'striking' modulations, varied 'figurations,' or effeminate 'melodies,'--none of those powerless, confusing rushes of instrumentation, the object of which is to benumb the intelligence of the listeners so that they may not detect the emptiness of this music. Hence it is that only the works of the masters just mentioned (and of the few in more recent times, who, like them, have remained true servants of that faithful 'Church' which exists no more here below), truly elevate and edify pious souls. Let me here mention the glorious master Fasch, who belongs to the old pious times, and whose profound and reverent writings have found so little favour with the frivolous crowd that his Mass for sixteen voices could not be published for want of due support. You would do me much injustice, Theodore, if you supposed that my mind is shut up with reference to the more modern music. Haydn, Mozart, and Beethoven have, in very truth, unfolded a new art, whose germ, perhaps, began to show itself in the middle of the eighteenth century. It was not the fault of those masters that frivolity and lack of comprehension prized the treasures already in existence so lightly that coiners of false money tried to give to their base metal the semblance of true currency. It is true that nearly in the same degree in which instrumental music gained in importance, vocal music became neglected, and that the complete disappearance of the true old choral music (which the result of sundry ecclesiastical changes--dissolution of the monasteries, and so forth), kept pace therewith. Of course it is quite clear that, now, it is not possible to go back to Palestrina's simplicity and grandeur, but it is still a question how far our new gains and progress can be brought into use in churches. The spirit which rules this world drives onward and onward continually; and although the forms which are lost and gone can never come back just as they were when they moved in our life-atmosphere, what is true is everlasting, imperishable, immortal; and a wondrous spiritual communion gently binds a mysterious band around

26

the past, the present, and the future. The sublime old masters are still alive, in the spirit. 'They being dead, yet speak.' Their music has not died away into silence, although in the roaring, tumultuous strife of the ungovernable which has broken in upon us, it is difficult to hear it. May the time of the fulfilling of our hopes be not far off! May a life of piety, peace, and joy begin, when Music, plying her Seraph-pinions freely and joyously once more, may enter upon her flight to the life beyond this, to that world which is her home, and whence comfort and salvation beam down into the unresting hearts of men."

Cyprian spoke those words with an unction which showed that they came truly from his heart of hearts. The friends, deeply moved by them, kept silence for some moments.

Then Sylvester said, "Although I am not a musician as Theodore and Cyprian are, I can assure you that I have thoroughly followed all you have said about Beethoven's Mass, and Church music in general. But, just as Cyprian complains that it may almost be said that there is no such person in existence at the present moment as a genuine ecclesiastical composer, I think I might assert that it would be hard to find a poet able to write worthy words for a Church composition."

"Quite true," said Theodore; "and the German words published with this very Mass of Beethoven's are but too clear a proof of it."

"But now," said Vincenz, rising from his chair, "like a second irate Pope Marcellus, I banish all further talk about music from the chapel of the Holy Saint Serapion. Both Theodore and Cyprian have spoken very finely, but let me move 'the previous question'--let us return to the strict rule of the Order, for which I, being a novice, am a great stickler."

"Vincenz is right," said Theodore. "Our dissertations have not been very interesting to the unskilled in music, wherefore it is well to bring them to a conclusion. Let Sylvester read us the tale he has brought with him."

This was agreed to, and Sylvester began, without further prelude, as follows:--

www.ingramcontent.com/pod-product-compliance
Lightning Source LLC
Chambersburg PA
CBHW030544180626
46810CB00005B/2005

* 9 7 8 1 4 4 7 4 6 5 5 7 7 *